PIGLET
TO THE RESCUE

DISNEY'S
POOH AND FRIENDS

by Ronald Kidd
illustrated by Vaccaro Associates, Inc.

Grolier Books

Based on the Pooh stories by A.A. Milne
[copyright the Pooh Properties Trust].

Edited by Ruth Lerner Perle
Produced by Graymont Enterprises, Inc.
Design and Art Direction by Michele Italiano-Perla
Pencil Layouts by Ennis McNulty
Painted by Lou Paleno

ISBN 0-7172-8444-1

Printed in the United States of America.

It was a blustery day in the Hundred-Acre Wood. The breeze dipped and swirled, stirring up leaves and making the branches shiver.

In the meadow, a very small animal made his way through the grass, leaning into the wind. It was Piglet, and he was dragging a kite behind him.

When Piglet got to the center of the meadow, he stopped and made sure the kite string wasn't tangled. Then he held the kite up into the breeze and let it go.

The kite jumped from Piglet's hand. It took off into the air and sailed over the treetops.

So did Piglet.

He was so small that the kite had lifted him right off the ground!

Piglet clung tightly to the string, looking down at the trees below.

"Oh, d-d-dear!" he whimpered. "Now what am I going to do?"

At that moment, in another part of the forest, Winnie the Pooh was asking himself that same question. "Now what am I going to do?"

Unlike Piglet, Pooh felt sure the answer would have something to do with honey. So he took a jar of honey from his cupboard and went outside.

Pooh looked at the honey jar, trying to decide from which side to sip. It was an important decision, and Pooh didn't like to rush into such things.

4

A voice called out, "Pooh! Winnie the Pooh!"

Pooh sat back. Honey jars had called to him before, but never quite this loudly. He leaned over the jar and peered down inside.

"Hello?" he said.

"Pooh! Up here!" cried the voice.

Pooh looked up just in time to see Piglet fly by. "Hello, Piglet!" he called. "Would you care for some honey?"

Piglet didn't answer because he was too busy tumbling through the air.

Pooh waved good-bye, thinking how lovely it was that there were flying animals such as blue jays and butterflies and Piglets.

Pooh said to his honey jar, "Don't you think Piglet is flying higher than usual today?"

Then he didn't say anything at all, because Pooh was thinking a thought. The thought was that Piglet wasn't a flying animal. He was a walking animal.

7

Reluctantly, Pooh set his honey jar aside and hurried
off through the forest after Piglet.

A moment later, Pooh came to a clearing filled with low
bushes. In the bushes was a kite,
and beside the kite was Piglet.

"Hello, Piglet," said Pooh. "I'm glad to be looking down at you instead of up."

Piglet wasn't glad—he was mad! He jumped to his feet and stamped the ground, saying, "Why, oh, why do I have to be so small?"

9

Pooh had never thought of Piglet as being small. He thought of him as being Piglet. He started to say so, but Piglet was not finished.

"I'm so small," said Piglet, "that I can eat only half a piece of pie.

"I'm so small that I can't reach the shelf of my closet.

"I'm so small that I can't even fly a kite!"

"Weren't you just flying one?" asked Pooh.

"No," said Piglet. "The kite was flying me."

Piglet was so angry that he hopped up and down. Every time he hopped, the breeze blew him back a little farther, until he fell into the bushes once again.

Pooh helped Piglet up from the bushes, dusted him off, and walked home with him.

But Piglet's anger could not be brushed off quite so easily. It hung on for days, until everyone in the forest was talking about it and wondering what to do.

All Piglet did anymore was stay home thinking of the things he could do if only he were big. As he thought, he made up a song.

Oh, I could be bigger,
As bigger as Tigger,
If only I weren't so small.

And I could be high, too,
As high as my friend, Pooh,
If I were not short, but tall.

Then, one afternoon, Piglet arrived at Pooh's house with a smile on his face.

"Pooh," he said, "you are looking at a brand-new animal!" Pooh tried to think what kind of animal it might be. He often did his best thinking while eating a jar of honey, and so he said to the brand-new animal, "Would you care to join me in a little something?"

13

"I don't want a little something!" said the animal. "I want a big something, to go with the kind of animal I am."

"What kind is that?" asked Pooh.

"A *biglet*."

"What's a biglet?" asked Pooh.

"It's like a piglet, only bigger," said Biglet.

Being a good host, Pooh went into his house and got the largest jar of honey he could find. Then the two of them sat down together and had a big something to eat.

Word about the brand-new animal spread through the forest, so Biglet had a lot of questions to answer.

Tigger asked, "How tall will you grow, Biglet?"

Biglet answered, "Taller than you can bounce!"

Christopher Robin asked, "When you get to be tall, will we still be friends?"

Biglet answered, "Of course! Biglets have big hearts."

Rabbit asked, "Piglet, how can you be so silly?"

Biglet didn't answer because Rabbit was talking to someone named Piglet.

Biglet said, "Excuse me, but I'd better be going now."

16

As Biglet hurried away, he met Kanga coming in the other direction.

"Have you seen Roo?" she asked. "He was playing outside, and now I can't find him anywhere. I'm worried because it will be dark soon."

Large creatures such as biglets like to solve problems all by themselves. But sometimes even they need to ask for help. This was one of those times.

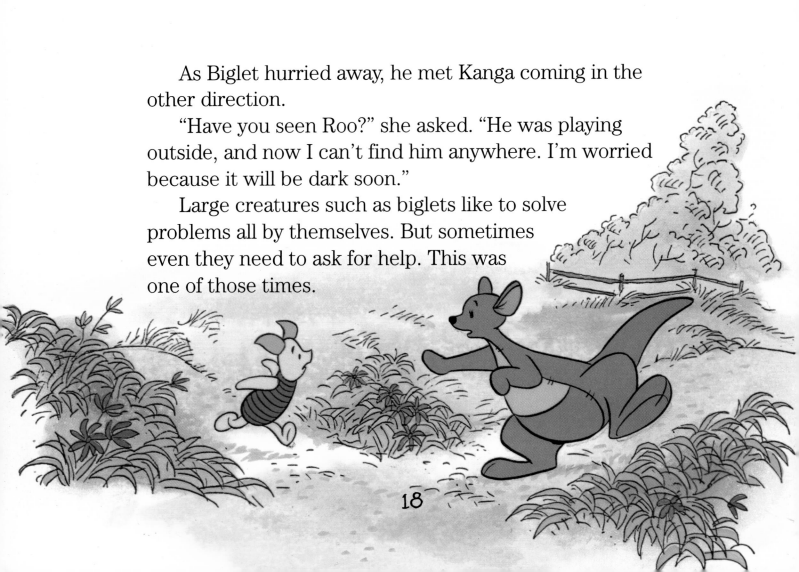

Biglet and Kanga found Christopher Robin and told him about Roo.

Within minutes, Christopher Robin had organized a search party to check every part of the forest.

The part Biglet was supposed to check was Six Pine Trees. He had gotten as far as the fourth pine tree when he heard a faint cry.

Biglet followed the cry to Pooh's heffalump trap, which was very much like a deep hole in the ground.

Biglet looked inside, and there was Roo at the bottom.

"Hello, Roo," said Biglet. "I'm here to save you."

"Yippee!" cried Roo.

Biglet called to Christopher Robin and the others, and soon all of them were standing around the heffalump trap.

Christopher Robin said, "Someone must go down into the trap and tie a rope around Roo. Then we can pull both of them out."

Everyone agreed it was a fine idea. The only question was who would go down.

Biglet said, "What's needed is a great big animal."

"A big animal could go down into the trap," said Christopher Robin, "but he would be too heavy to pull out. What's really needed is a small animal."

Everyone looked at Biglet.

Biglet asked, "How about Rabbit?"
Nobody said anything.
"Pooh is small," said Biglet. "At least, parts of him are.
Kanga said, "No, the only one small enough and brave enough is Piglet."

"If only Piglet were here," said Christopher Robin. "Then he could rescue poor little Roo."

Biglet thought of all his big plans. He had wanted a big house and big food and big adventures. Then he thought of little Roo stuck at the bottom of the heffalump trap.

24

Biglet sighed and said, "Oh, well. Perhaps it's not so bad being a piglet."

Piglet climbed down the side of the trap. He tied one end of the rope around Roo. Then he tugged on the rope, and the others pulled them up out of the trap.

Roo was safe!

Kanga gathered Roo in one arm and Piglet in the other.

"Big things are nice," she said, hugging them both. "But sometimes the best things are the smallest."

Piglet's friends cheered. Pooh lifted Piglet to his shoulders and then everyone paraded to Pooh's house, where they had a wonderful party now that Roo . . . and Piglet were back home again.

Christopher Robin sat at one end of the table, and at the other end sat the guest of honor—the hero whose name wasn't Biglet, but Piglet. He was so small that he could barely see over the table. But today that didn't bother him at all.